What's In That Cat's Ear?

Written & Illustrated by:

Anne N Buffington

ISBN: 1480094048
ISBN-13: 9781480094048

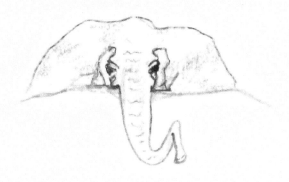

This Book is dedicated to my dear Friend,

Howard,

who told me a charming
Story about his boyhood years,
When his Grandfather left him in on
A secret.

Something very special lives in
The cat's ear.

Howard believed the story throughout
his entire boyhood.

To all who have vivid imaginations,
may this story act as inspiration.

Listen, listen I have a story to tell
Of a cat, a witch and a magical spell.
The story to tell is about the cat's ear
And the spell that got cast
on the poor little dear.

*Did you know there is something
living in the cat ear?
Yes, that is true, quite true I fear.*

That something is
lumpy, bumpy and gray
And it has a long trunk
so they say.

What do you think it
could possibly be ...
A bird, a bug,
a frog or a bee?

No it's an animal very big
... very gray
I don't think you could
guess it if you took all day.
So I will give you a few
more clues ...
It can live in a circus ...
also a zoo
And many times in a
jungle too.

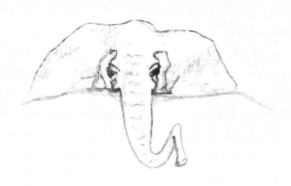

I can't believe it yet it's
so very clear ...
Are you telling me an
elephant lives
in the cat's ear?
Yes, it is true ... so true
... I fear.

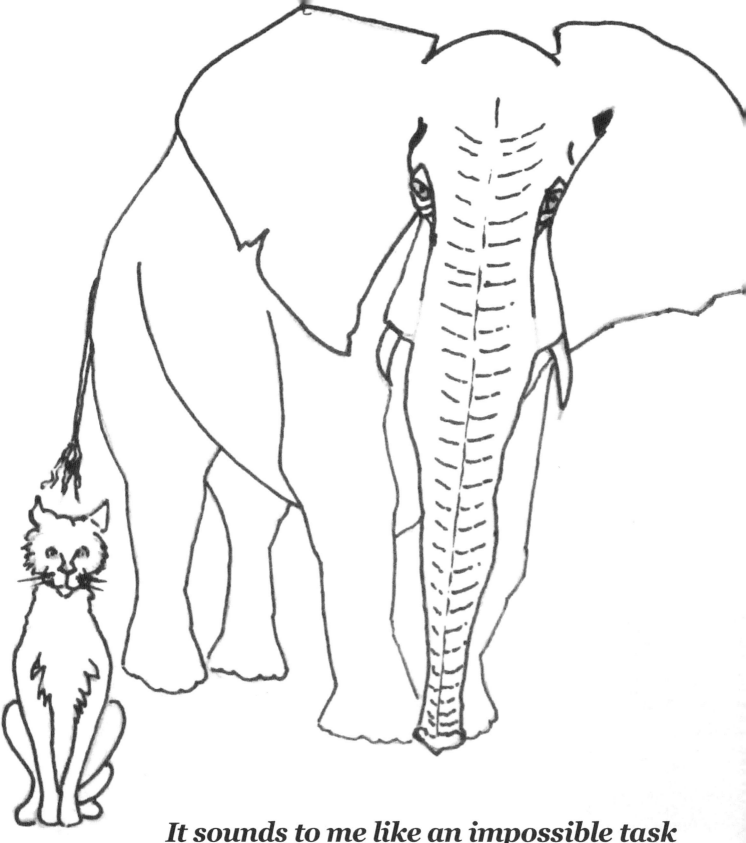

It sounds to me like an impossible task

How in the world could this be I ask?

We all know the cat is so little so very small ...

The elephant is so big, so very tall ...

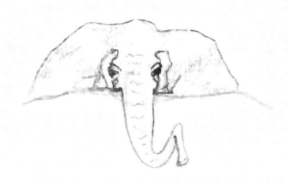

I will tell you the story as
it was told to me
Then you'll understand
how this came to be.
One warm, sunny day the
cat was taking a stroll
Through a very beautiful
and charming
country knoll.

A teeny, tiny, witch
named Tillie
was strolling too
But the cat was so
busy admiring the view
He accidentally
knocked Tillie,
the teeny, tiny, witch
into a very deep,
deep ditch,

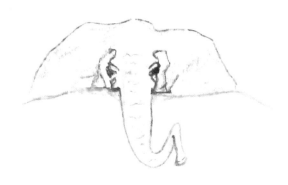

Tillie tried but could not
climb out of the Ditch ...
This made her so mad she
started to Twitch ...
And to make matters
worse also to itch.
Furious, she shook her
fist at the cat
And shouted for this
insult she
Would pay the cat back.

The frightened cat exclaimed,
"Now What do I do?
I can't get the witch out of the
ditch ... that is true."

So the cat cried out,
could someone
Please help me?
The elephant heard
the cat's cries
and arrived on the
scene.

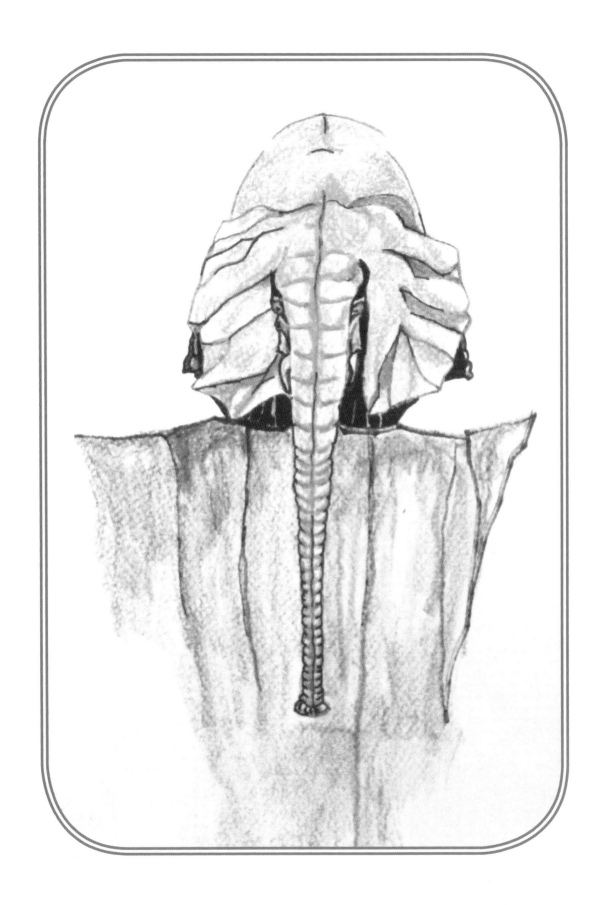

To rescue the witch he planned to dunk
His head into the ditch and pull her out by his trunk.

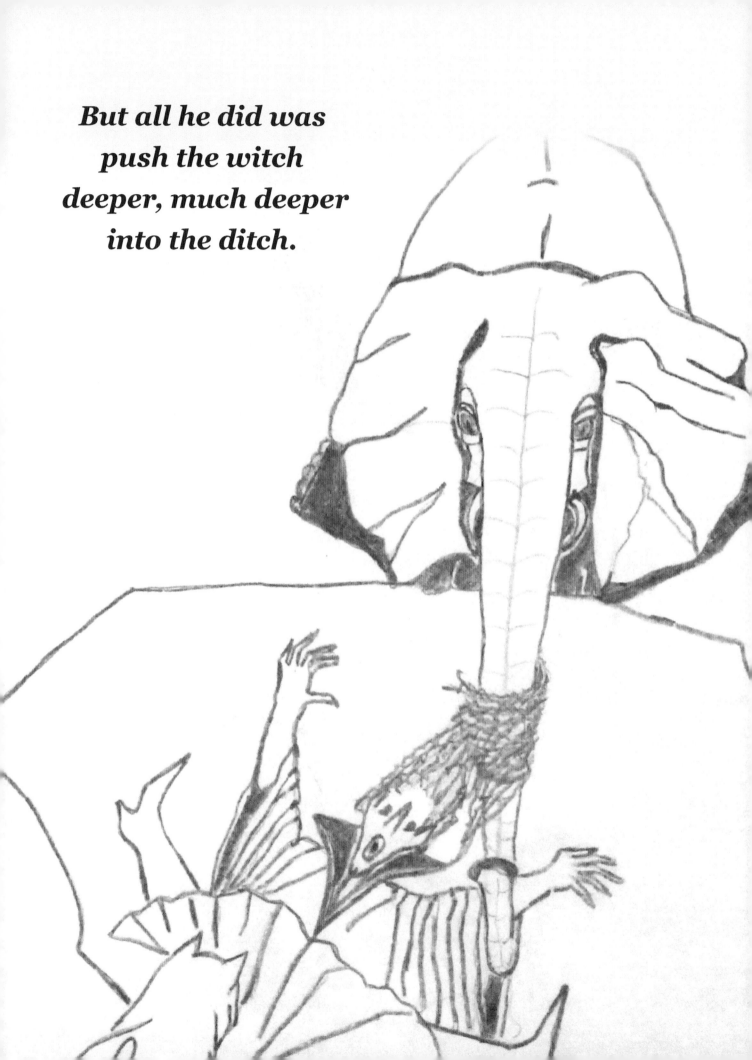

But all he did was push the witch deeper, much deeper into the ditch.

**This made Tillie even madder
so she blamed the Elephant too
He became so upset, he turned a bright blue.**

Right then and there Tillie
decided to brew up a curse
She had a new recipe she
would try out first.
With a snap of her fingers,
the cauldron appeared
Lickity split and her
ingredients were
There.

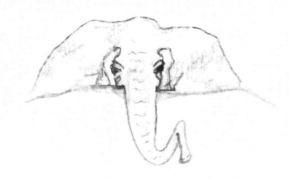

She stirred and
stirred and brewed
all kinds of things
Herbs and strange
flowers and butterfly
wings.

And just to make sure is was an extra nasty brew
She added a large pinch of magic dust too.

The cat and the elephant looked on with great fear
They were so scared they were frozen there.

Finally, it was time for Tillie to cast her spell
It was a wicked brew she could tell.
She knew at once what she would do
She took the wand and dipped it into the brew

And she said to herself,
I'll make him as small as me
Not much bigger than a garden pea.

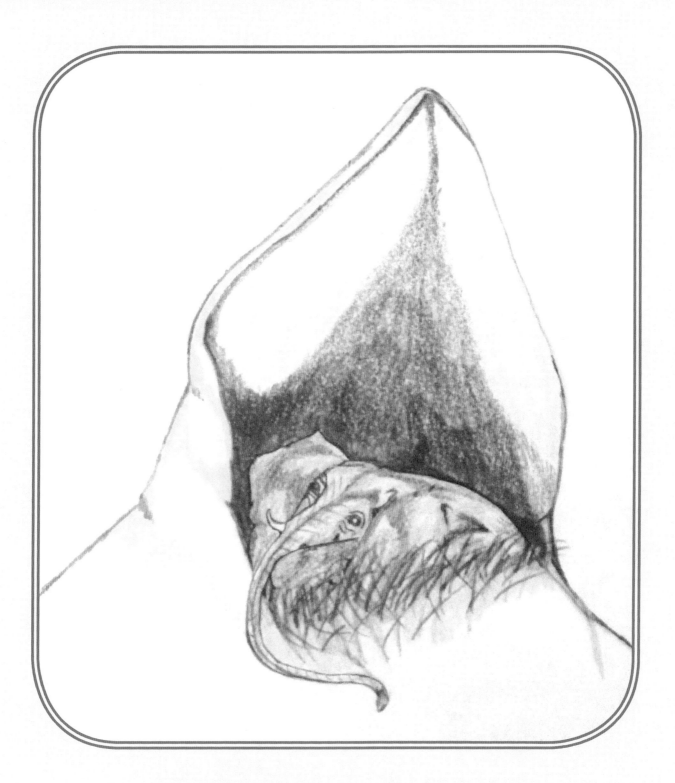

Next, she waved her wand at
The cat's ear ...
And poor elephant landed in it
as Tillie laughed
and cheered.

And then she did what all witches do
Called for her dragonfly and off she flew.

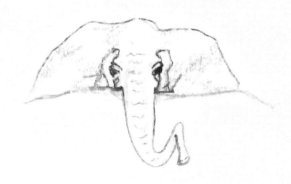

The poor cat moaned ... "
Now what do I
Do ..
Poor Elephant's stuck in my ear
Me-Yew ... Me-Yew.

Oh Elephant, Elephant what can I
Say ...
This has been just a terrible day.
I don't know how to get you
Out of my ear ...
I must think about it ... it may take a year.

The elephant replied ... "Don't worry
My friend ...
It is so nice in here, I know I
Could spend ...
My lifetime in here enjoying the
View ...
Furthermore, it is comfortable too.

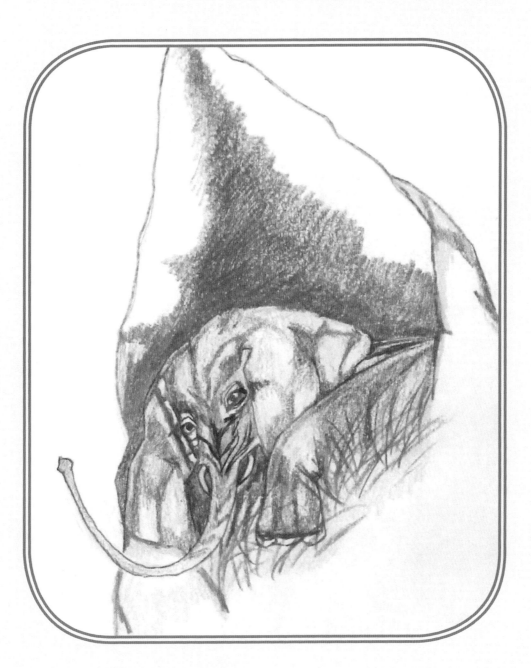

How would you feel if I wanted to
Stay
In here forever ... forever and a day.

Well, this is a surprising turn of events.
I'll let you stay and won't charge
You rent.

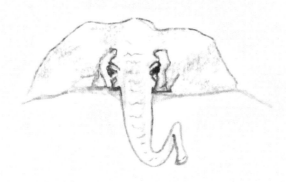

As far as I know to this very
Day ...
They are living together ... that's
What they say.

So the next time you see a cat
Whisper in his ear ...
Hello, Mr. Elephant, so glad you are
Here.

Isn't it also wonderful as well ...
That Tillie's brew cast a happy spell?
I know you could tell Tillie, the
Teeny tiny witch ...
Always knew how to get out of
That ditch.

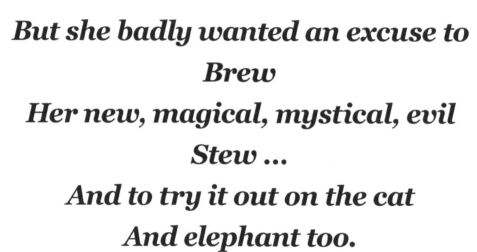

But she badly wanted an excuse to
Brew
Her new, magical, mystical, evil
Stew ...
And to try it out on the cat
And elephant too.

But her new recipe had one
Big flaw ...
Instead of butterfly wings she
Should have used bear claws.
The butterfly wings put happiness
Into the brew ...
But it was too late by the time she knew.

I would like to end this story
So sweet
By telling you a secret you can't repeat …
The next time you see a cat groom
His ear …
He's saying, "wake up Mr. Elephant
I'm here … I'm here.
How are you feeling on this fine,
Sunny day …

Let's go out in the yard and play
And play.

The cat and the elephant are the best
Of friends ...

And that is how this story ends.

The end.

THE CAT

*The cat lives in a cottage at the
edge of the woods.
His life is full of all that is good.
One of his special treats is cream
and he always licks his bowl clean.
He frolics and plays all day long
chases bugs, birds and frogs by
the pond.
He also likes to take lots of naps
His favorite spot is his owners lap.*

THE ELEPHANT

The elephant lives in a petting zoo
He loves the children, but the zoo makes him blue.
Because elephants love to wander and roam
travel many miles and call many places home.
So elephant learned how to escape from the zoo
The owners were upset but didn't know what to do.
The last time he escaped, he disappeared
vanished in thin air ... it is all so weird.
They have no idea where he could be
to this day it is a mystery.

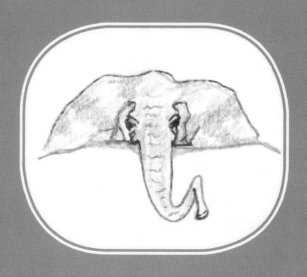

TILLIE, THE WITCH

*Tillie, the teeny, tiny witch has red curly hair
which does not fit
into what most consider to look like a witch.
To make matters worse she is very small
If you don't look close you wouldn't see her at all.
A broom is too big, so a dragonfly she rides
but he loves ponds and waters rather than hill sides.
She never seems to get her witches brews right
even when she tries with all of her might.
They start out bad as bad as can be
but end up being good brews, unhappily.
There are many more stories to tell
about Tillie, the teeny, tiny witch and her spells.
So you will be hearing about her once again ...
of her many misadventures that never seem to end.*

Made in the USA
Charleston, SC
17 May 2013